IF I MET AN ICE AGE ANIMAL

IF I WANDERED WITH A WOOLLY MAMMOTH

by Jenna Lee Gleisner
illustrated by Michelle Simpson

GRASSHOPPER

Tools for Parents & Teachers

Grasshopper Books enhance imagination and introduce the earliest readers to fiction with fun storylines and illustrations. The easy-to-read text supports early reading experiences with repetitive sentence patterns and sight words.

Before Reading

- Discuss the cover illustration. What do readers see?
- Look at the picture glossary together. Discuss the words.

Read the Book

- Read the book to the child, or have him or her read independently.
- "Walk" through the book and look at the illustrations. Who is the main character? What is happening in the story?

After Reading

- Prompt the child to think more. Ask: The main character imagines wandering with woolly mammoths during the Ice Age. What do you think it would be like to live in the Ice Age?

Grasshopper Books are published by Jump!
5357 Penn Avenue South
Minneapolis, MN 55419
www.jumplibrary.com

Library of Congress Cataloging-in-Publication Data

Names: Gleisner, Jenna Lee, author.
Simpson, Michelle (Illustrator), illustrator.
Title: If I wandered with a woolly mammoth
by Jenna Lee Gleisner; illustrated by Michelle Simpson.
Description: Minneapolis, MN: Jump!, Inc., 2023.
Series: If I met an Ice Age animal | Includes index.
Audience: Ages 5-8.
Identifiers: LCCN 2021060800 (print)
LCCN 2021060801 (ebook)
ISBN 9781636909547 (hardcover)
ISBN 9781636909554 (paperback)
ISBN 9781636909561 (ebook)
Subjects: CYAC: Woolly mammoth–Fiction.
Mammoths–Fiction. | Prehistoric animals–Fiction.
LCGFT: Picture books.
Classification: LCC PZ7.1.G5885 Ifp 2023 (print)
LCC PZ7.1.G5885 (ebook)
DDC [E]–dc23
LC record available at https://lccn.loc.gov/2021060800
LC ebook record available at https://lccn.loc.gov/2021060801

Editor: Eliza Leahy
Direction and Layout: Anna Peterson
Illustrator: Michelle Simpson

Printed in the United States of America at
Corporate Graphics in North Mankato, Minnesota.

Table of Contents

Woolly Wanderers

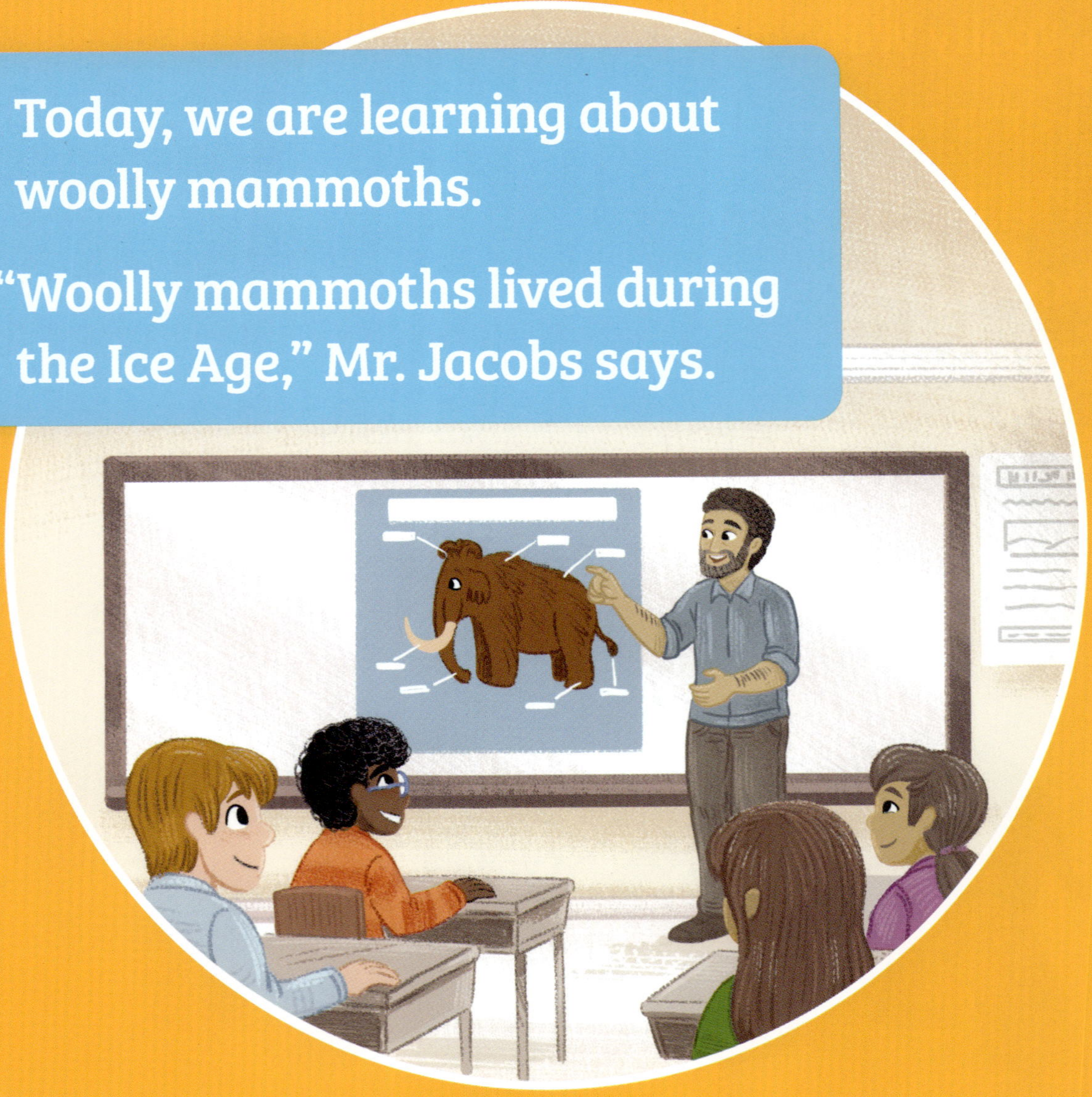

Today, we are learning about woolly mammoths.

"Woolly mammoths lived during the Ice Age," Mr. Jacobs says.

What if I wandered with a woolly mammoth? I wonder.

If I wandered with a woolly mammoth, I'd have to bundle up. I would need a winter jacket, hat, and mittens. I'd need snow boots, too. I am in the Ice Age after all!

The woolly mammoth, though? I'll call him Mack. Mack has a thick coat of hair to keep him warm.

If I got cold, I'd wrap myself in Mack's hair. Woolly mammoth hair was long!

If I wandered with a woolly mammoth, I'd watch my step. Mack's giant feet could squish me in an instant!

If I wandered with Mack, I'd also watch out for his friends. Woolly mammoths traveled in herds.

herd

If I wandered with woolly mammoths, I wouldn't get tired. Why? I could ride on Mack's back. He's so tall he can get through snow with no problem!

Or I could sit on one of his tusks!

If I wandered with Mack,
I wouldn't have to find food.
His trunk sniffs for it. He uses
his long tusks to dig up grass
for us to eat.

trunk

If I wandered with woolly mammoths, I'd be safe. Mack would protect me from predators like saber-toothed cats.

Just then, something catches my eye.

It is snowing outside!

Mr. Jacobs goes on. “But woolly mammoths and other Ice Age animals have been extinct for more than 10,000 years. What would you do if you saw a woolly mammoth?”

Parts of a Woolly Mammoth

Woolly mammoths weighed more than six tons (5,400 kilograms). They were up to 13 feet (4.0 meters) tall. Take a look at the parts of a woolly mammoth.

Picture Glossary

coat
An animal's covering of hair or fur.

extinct
No longer found alive and known about only through fossils or history.

herds
Large numbers of animals that stay or move together.

Ice Age
A period of time, about 10,000 years ago, when a large part of Earth was covered with ice.

predators
Animals that hunt other animals for food.

wandered
Moved around without a particular purpose. If your mind wanders, it means you are distracted.

Index

To Learn More

FACT SURFER

Finding more information is as easy as 1, 2, 3.

1. Go to www.factsurfer.com
2. Enter "**ifIwanderedwithawoollymammoth**" into the search box.
3. Choose your book to see a list of websites.